Before I Say Goodnight

Julia Porter

Illustrated by Patricia Pearsall

KPk
Key Porter Kids

Royalties from the sale of this book will benefit the Make-A-Wish Foundation® of Canada.

National Library of Canada Cataloguing in Publication Data

Porter, Julia, 1977-
            Before I say goodnight

ISBN 1-55263-373-X

I. Pearsall, Patricia II. Title

PS8581.O75718B44 2001   jC813i.6   C2001-901676-X
PZ.P8175Be 2001

The Canada Council | Le Conseil des Arts
FOR THE ARTS | DU CANADA
SINCE 1957 | DEPUIS 1957   ONTARIO ARTS COUNCIL
                                CONSEIL DES ARTS DE L'ONTARIO

The publisher gratefully acknowledges the support of the Canada Council for the Arts and the Ontario Arts Council for its publishing program.

We acknowledge the financial support of the Government of Canada through the Book Publishing Industry Development Program (BPIDP) for our publishing activities.

Key Porter Books Limited
70 The Esplanade
Toronto, Ontario
Canada M5E 1R2
www.keyporter.com

Design: Patricia Cavazzini
Printed and bound in Canada
01 02 03 04 05 06   6 5 4 3 2 1

Before I say "goodnight" this night,
I'll shut my eyes and close them tight.
I'll think of all the things I've done,
All before the setting sun.

Remember all the games I've played,
The funny faces I have made.
All the people I have seen,
All the places I have been.
All the crazy things I've said,
As I am tucked into my bed.

I'll puff my pillow nice and round,
Imagine every kind of sound.
From chirping birds to swaying trees,

Laughing kids and splashing seas,
Music from the ice cream truck,
A hockey rink – a sliding puck.

I'll set my dreams up perfectly,
With ANY me I want to be.
Picture puddles, rubber boots,

Slipping into chocolate suits,
Doing hand stands through the town,
Then flying high and up-side-down.

I'll walk through candy factories,
I'll swing from giant cherry trees.

Sidewalks will be trampolines,
There won't be any lima beans.

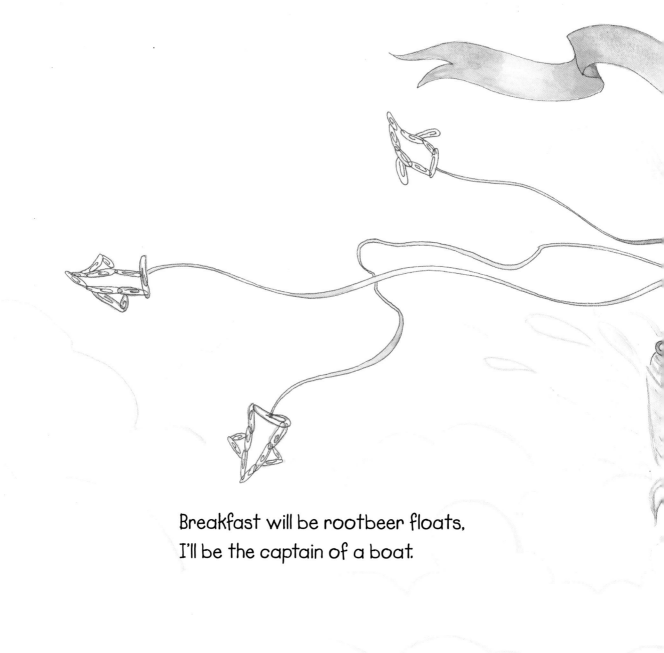

Breakfast will be rootbeer floats,
I'll be the captain of a boat.

Or the head of my own space ship,
Made of glue and paperclips.

I'll visit fairies in far-off lands,
Where swings are made of rubber bands.
And see-saws made of ball-point pens,
And slides from straws that twist and bend.

Next I'll fly with brand new wings,
To visit famous Queens and Kings.
To dance among their daisy fields,
To try on all their royal shields.

Then head off for another trip,
Upon a golden sea-bound ship.

Toward a land of reds and greens,
All the bright blues you've ever seen.
With orange sky and trees so yellow,
And purple heads on every fellow.

Where girls are covered in polka-dots,
Instead of hats, they all wear pots.
They laugh at every joke I say,
And always have a game to play.

I'll stay with them for quite a while,
Walking every way but single-file.

We'll dance on lemon treetops,

We'll belly flop in purple pools.

We'll somersault down turquoise hills,

Have puppet shows on windowsills.

From there I'm not sure where I'll go,
When I wake up I'll let you know,

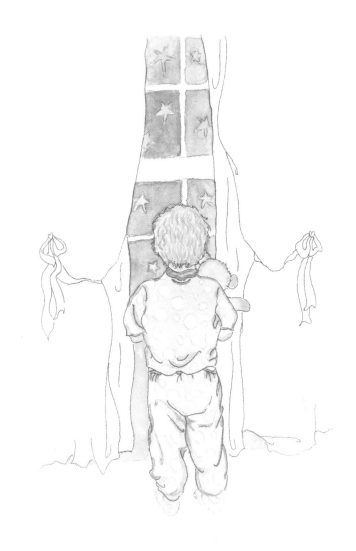

But first I have to fall asleep,
Shut my eyes, not make a peep.
Drift to a dreamland pure and true,
Do ANYTHING I want to do.

So kiss me once, and hug me tight,
And then go ahead – turn off the light.
My dreams are ready to take flight.
Oh! And don't forget to say "Goodnight."